Everyone is scared of something.

Living with fear can make even the bravest person feel small.

Emily Gravett's
Big Book
of Fears

is *the* essential book to help you overcome your phobias.

It has been put together by an expert in worrying,
who draws on a lifetime's experience of managing
her fears through the medium of doodle.

You too can overcome your fears through the use of art!

Each page in this book provides a large blank space
for you to record and face your fear using a combination of:
Drawing
Writing
Collage.

REMEMBER!
A FEAR FACED IS A FEAR DEFEATED.

First published 2007 by Macmillan Children's Books
This edition published 2008 by Macmillan Children's Books
an imprint of Pan Macmillan,
20 New Wharf Road, London N1 9RR
www.panmacmillan.com

ISBN: 978-0-230-01619-4

11 13 15 14 12 10

A CIP catalogue record for this book is available from the British Library.

Printed in China

Little Mouse's

~~Emily Gravett's~~

Big Book

of

Fears

MACMILLAN CHILDREN'S BOOKS

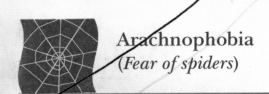

Arachnophobia
(Fear of spiders)

Use the space below to record your fears.

I'm scared

of creepy crawlies

(especially spiders!).

Entomophobia
(*Fear of insects*)

Use the space below to record your fears.

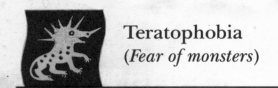

Teratophobia
(Fear of monsters)

Use the space below to record your fears.

I worry about what's under the bed.

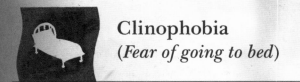

Clinophobia
(*Fear of going to bed*)

Use the space below to record your fears.

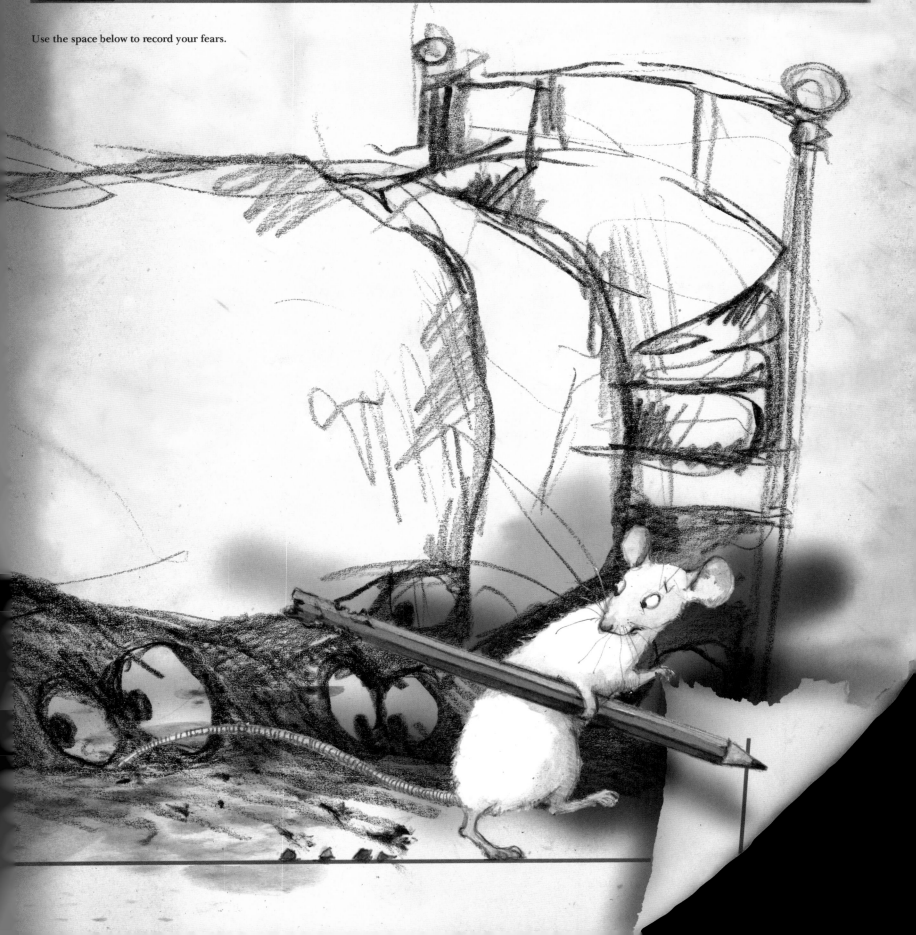

Aichmophobia
(Fear of knives)

Use the space below to record your fears.

I get edgy near sharp knives.

Get Well Soon

THE AMAZING FLYING
MOUSECROBATS
CIRCUS
CANCELLED

DID YOU EVER SEE SUCH A THING IN YOUR LIFE?

THE AMAZING MOUSECROBAT TRIO ARE COMPLETELY BLIND!
SEE HOW THEY PERFORM USING ONLY THEIR TAILS AND SENSE OF SMELL
TO GUIDE THEM!

THREE BLIND MICE

The Farmer's Friend

News, views and moos from down on the farm

The Farmer's Friend

Mouse numb

Tail End for Deep Cut Farm's Mouse Problem

by M Ferguson

Deep Cut Farm of Lower Wallop is enjoying its first mouse-free evening for weeks after a recent assault by a trio of cheese-mad rodents made life intolerable on the once peaceful dairy farm.

Matters came to a head last Saturday when Mrs Sabatier, wife of Farmer Sabatier, (Best Big Cheese Award Winner 2005) decided that enough was enough.

"The blinking mice had been driving me mad! They was running after me while I was working. I think they could smell the cheese!" she fumed. "I just lost it, I was blind mad! I picked up the nearest thing to hand, which was my carving knife, and before I knew what I had done, there were three tails in my hand, and three mice running as fast as their legs could carry them out of the door."

Well, one thing's for certain, that's the last time those three

Mrs Sabatier triumphan

Find an Expert

AMAZING

C
IS
that, due to un
performanc
per

Ablutophobia
(*Fear of bathing*)

Use the space below to record your fears.

I'm frightened I may

get sucked down the

plughole

Hydrophobia
(Fear of water)

Use the space below to record your fears.

Use the space below to

Rupophobia
(*Fear of dirt*)

Use the space below to record your fears.

I worry about having accidents.

Ligyrophobia
(Fear of loud noises)

I'M ALARMED BY

HICKORY

Hickory Dicko
The mou
The clock str
The m
Hick

Chronomentrophobia
(*Fear of clocks*)

LOUD NOISES!

ICKORY
ORY DOCK

A NEW SETTING
AN OLD RHYME
BY
ly Gravett
WITH
APOLOGIES
TO
NYO IN EARSHOT

the mouse ran up the clock   The clock struck one

down   Hick-o-ry dick-o-ry dock
9094

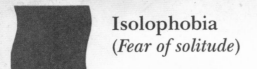

Isolophobia
(Fear of solitude)

Use the space below to record your fears.

I don't like being alone, or in the dark.

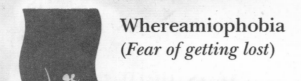

Whereamiophobia
(Fear of getting lost)

Use the space below to record your fears.

I'm scared of getting lost. . . . .

Phagophobia
(Fear of being eaten)

Use the space below to record your fears.

WOOF!

Cynophobia
(Fear of dogs)

Use the space below to record your fears.

I get nervous near dogs.

Use the space below to record your

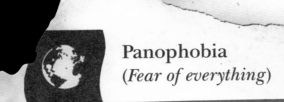

Panophobia
(Fear of everything)

Use the space below to record your fears.

I'm afraid of nearly EVERYTHING I see.

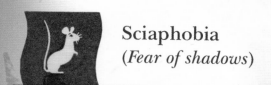

Sciaphobia
(*Fear of shadows*)

Use the space below to record your fears.

But even though
I'm very
small...

Use the space below to record your fears.

she's afraid of

ME !

Bibliophobia
(Fear of books)

Use the space below to record your fears.

This book is dedicated to anyone who suffers from Musophobia. (Fear of mice)

The fabulous rats Button and Mr. Moo, who taught me everything I know about nibbling.

BIG CHEESE BOOKS

Unit 3 Port Salut Shopping Centre Glouces...
BOOK TITLE
Gravett's Big Book of Fears

SEE HOW THEY PERFORM

Little Mouse

...rgh Hippopotomonstrosesquipped...
(Fear of long words)

EEEEEK

This is to certify that

. . . .

was
very
VERY
brave about

. . . .